J
358.4
R297

R.L. 4.2
PTS. 0.5
TST. 503130
LG

Brownstown Public Library
120 E. Spring St.
Brownstown IN 47220
(812) 358-2853

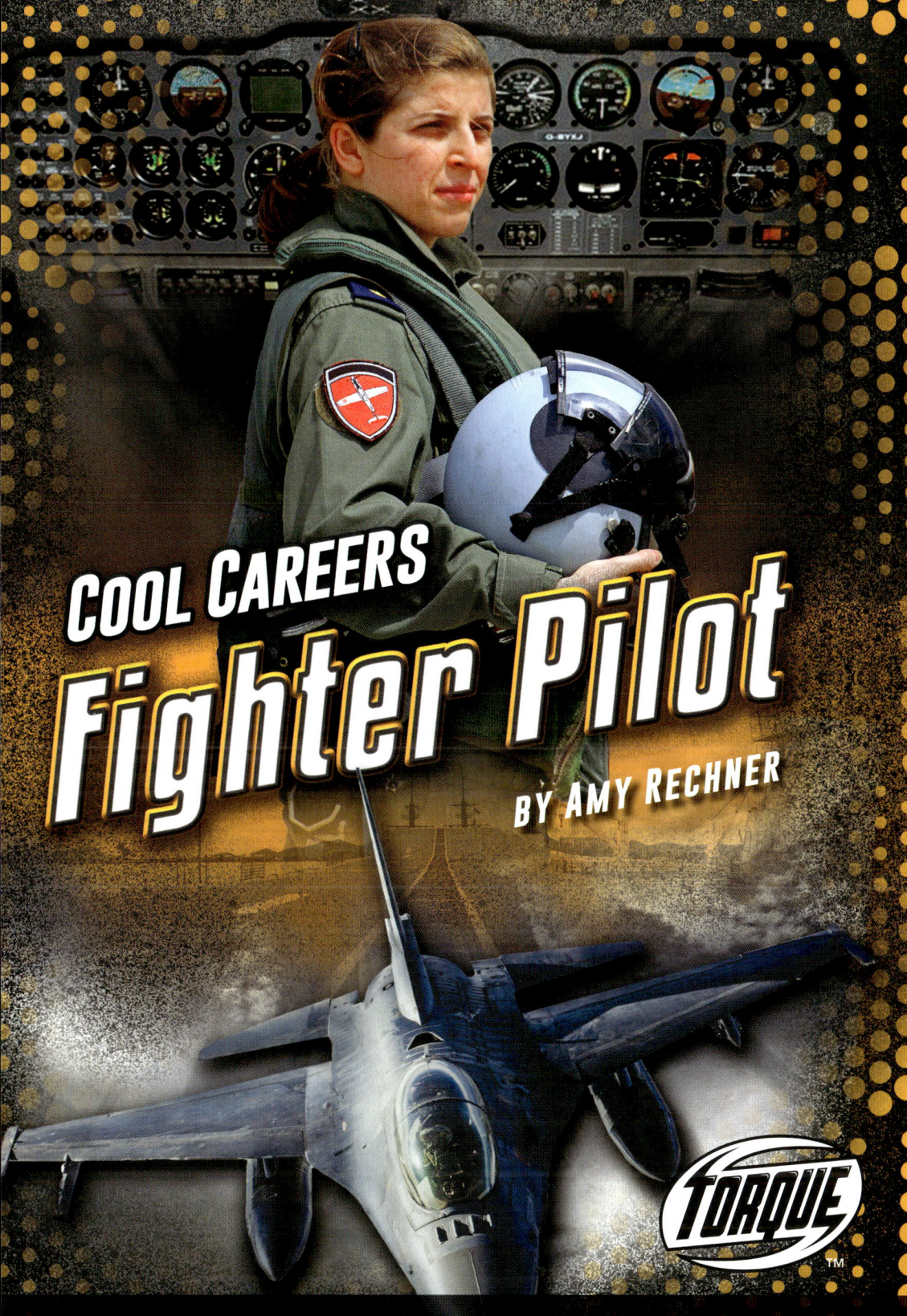

Are you ready to take it to the extreme? Torque books thrust you into the action-packed world of sports, vehicles, mystery, and adventure. These books may include dirt, smoke, fire, and dangerous stunts.

WARNING: read at your own risk.

This edition first published in 2020 by Bellwether Media, Inc.

No part of this publication may be reproduced in whole or in part without written permission of the publisher. For information regarding permission, write to Bellwether Media, Inc., Attention: Permissions Department, 6012 Blue Circle Drive, Minnetonka, MN 55343.

Library of Congress Cataloging-in-Publication Data

Names: Rechner, Amy, author.
Title: Fighter Pilot / by Amy Rechner.
Description: Minneapolis, MN : Bellwether Media, Inc., 2020. | Series: Torque:
   Cool Careers | Includes bibliographical references and index. |
   Audience: Ages: 7-12. | Audience: Grades: 3-7.
Identifiers: LCCN 2018061280 (print) | LCCN 2019004048 (ebook) | ISBN
   9781618916297 (ebook) | ISBN 9781644870624 (hardcover : alk. paper)
Subjects: LCSH: Fighter pilots–Juvenile literature. | Air warfare–Juvenile
   literature.
Classification: LCC UG631 (ebook) | LCC UG631 .R43 2020 (print) | DDC
   358.4/3023–dc23
LC record available at https://lccn.loc.gov/2018061280

Text copyright © 2020 by Bellwether Media, Inc. TORQUE and associated logos are trademarks and/or registered trademarks of Bellwether Media, Inc. SCHOLASTIC, CHILDREN'S PRESS, and associated logos are trademarks and/or registered trademarks of Scholastic Inc., 557 Broadway, New York, NY 10012.

Editor: Kate Moening   Designer: Josh Brink

Printed in the United States of America, North Mankato, MN.

TABLE OF CONTENTS

Tough Landing	4
On a Mission	6
Ready for Anything	10
A Pilot's Journey	18
Glossary	22
To Learn More	23
Index	24

Tough Landing

missile

The fighter pilot launches a **missile** at a target. Smoke and flames explode on the ground below. The pilot rolls his aircraft skyward and flies back to base with the other planes.

The aircraft carrier rocks on the ocean as the first plane approaches. Wheels meet the short 300-foot (91-meter) runway. The **wire trap** catches the plane's tail hook. The plane stops. A successful landing!

wire trap

On a Mission

Air Force fighter jets

Fighter pilots fly planes for the military. They fight from the air! They launch missiles and drop bombs on enemy targets.

In the United States, Air Force pilots do the most in-air fighting. Navy pilots patrol the air and look for enemy submarines. Marine pilots often support ground **missions**.

Navy fighter jet

A POWERFUL SLINGSHOT

Launching from a carrier is tricky. Powerful slingshots help shoot planes into the air!

aircraft carrier

Navy pilots live on aircraft carriers for months at a time. They train, study, and launch planes for missions. More than 6,000 people can live on an aircraft carrier!

Air Force pilots and their families live on bases around the world. A base is like a small town. Families live in houses. There are even schools and stores!

Famous Face
Tammie Jo Shults

BIRTHDAY: NOVEMBER 2, 1961

HOMETOWN: TULAROSA, NEW MEXICO

EDUCATION:
- AGRIBUSINESS AND BIOLOGY DEGREES (MID-AMERICA NAZARENE COLLEGE)
- UNITED STATES NAVY OFFICER CANDIDATE SCHOOL

ACHIEVEMENTS:
- ONE OF THE FIRST FEMALE PILOTS IN THE U.S. NAVY
- TRAINED FIGHTER PILOTS FOR COMBAT DURING OPERATION DESERT STORM
- SERVED IN NAVY RESERVE AND RECEIVED FOUR MEDALS
- AS A PILOT FOR SOUTHWEST AIRLINES, SHE CALMLY LANDED A FULL PLANE AFTER AN ENGINE EXPLODED IN MIDAIR, SAVING 148 LIVES

Ready for Anything

Fighter pilots have long checklists. These help the pilots make sure planes are ready to fly. Pilots go through the lists before every flight. There are more than 80 checklist items for the **cockpit** alone!

When pilots are called out to a mission, they **scramble** quickly. They must get in the air in less than five minutes!

During a mission, pilots fly out ready to fight. They battle in the air and strike targets on the ground. They fly low over enemy territory to do **surveillance**. They can quickly zoom away if they are spotted. Missions can last more than ten hours!

Back on the ground, pilots continue to train and study flight manuals. They must always be ready to go!

PUTTING ON A SHOW

Sometimes pilots perform flyovers at events like football games. The Air Force's Thunderbirds and the Navy's Blue Angels are special performance flight teams!

Practice Mission Checklist

- ☑ **4:30 AM:** WAKE UP

- ☑ **6:00 AM:** GO OVER MISSION GOALS WITH CREW

- ☑ **8:00 AM:** FINALIZE MISSION PLAN

- ☑ **9:00 AM:** SUIT UP; GO OVER CHECKLIST

- ☑ **10:00 AM:** MISSION TAKE-OFF

- ☑ **11:15 AM:** RETURN TO BASE

- ☑ **12:30 PM:** TALK ABOUT HOW THE MISSION WENT

- ☑ **4:00 PM:** GET READY TO DO EVERYTHING AGAIN TOMORROW!

MAKING STRONG PILOTS

Long-range weapons have made dogfighting less common. But training for dogfights makes stronger pilots who can handle stress.

practice dogfight

When pilots meet enemy planes, they may end up in a dogfight. Dogfighting is the common term for an air battle. Pilots avoid enemy fire with rolls and dives.

These moves create strong **g-forces**. G-forces at high **altitude** can make pilots sick! Pilots work together to get home safely.

BE PREPARED

Pilots wear vests with extra supplies in case they make a sudden landing. Vests may have radios, flares, matches, and even shark repellant!

vest with supplies

Pilots' work is full of danger. They have special gear to keep them safe from g-forces and other risks.

Special suits squeeze pilots' bodies tightly to keep blood flowing to the brain. They wear oxygen masks to breathe at high altitudes. If pilots **eject**, parachutes carry them to safety! Pilots' packs include floating life vests for water landings.

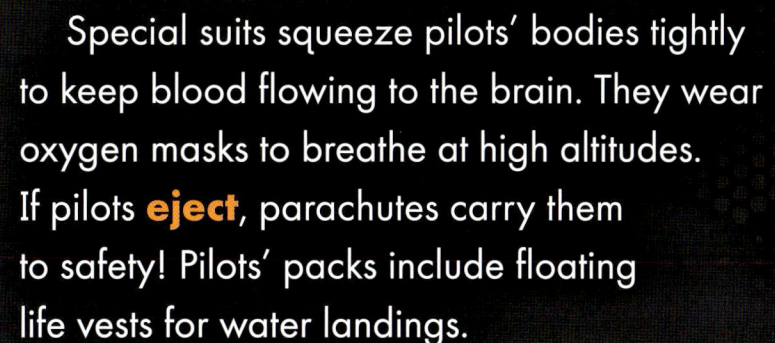

oxygen mask

A Pilot's Journey

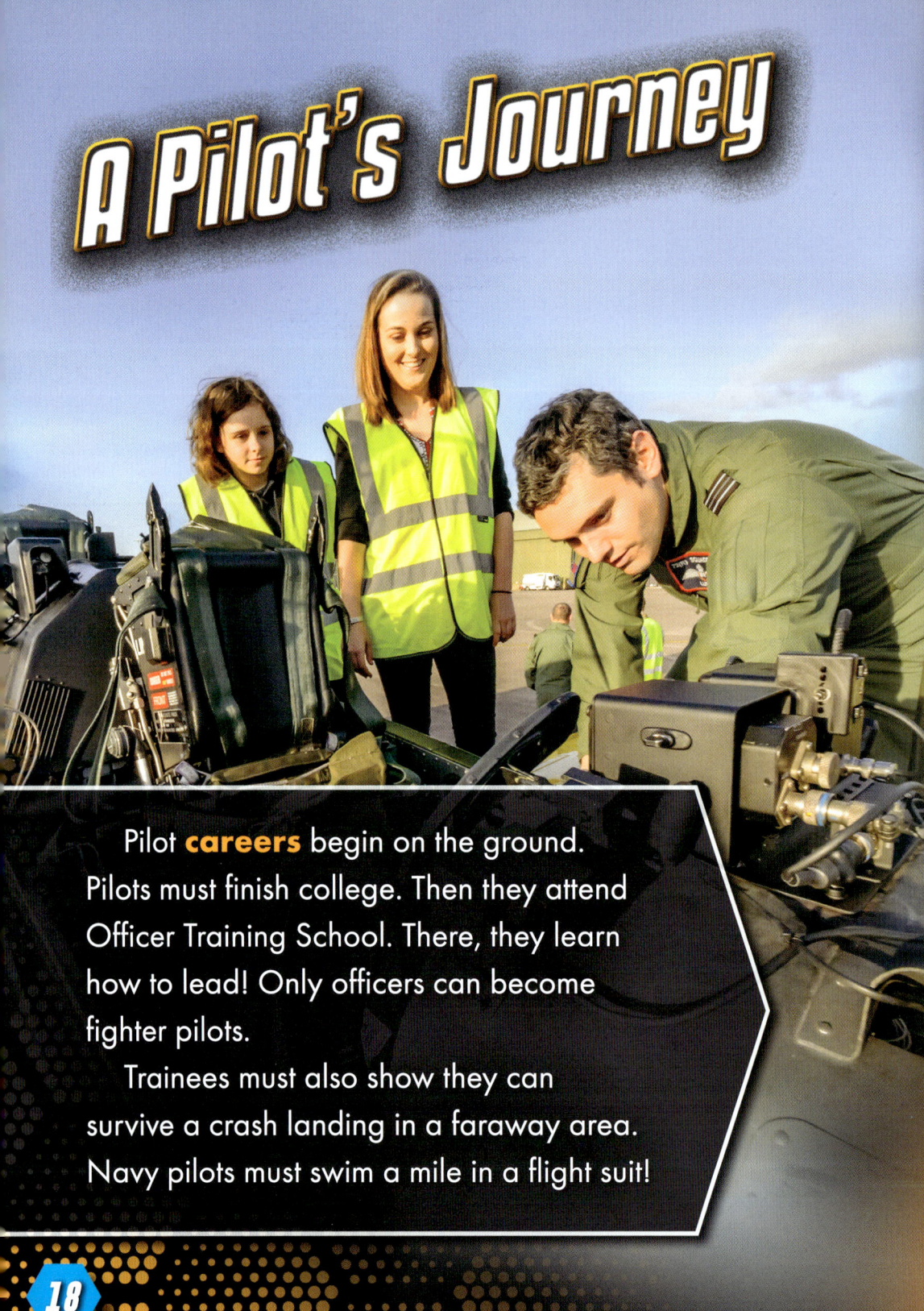

Pilot **careers** begin on the ground. Pilots must finish college. Then they attend Officer Training School. There, they learn how to lead! Only officers can become fighter pilots.

Trainees must also show they can survive a crash landing in a faraway area. Navy pilots must swim a mile in a flight suit!

Career Path

COLLEGE 4-6 YEARS

OFFICER TRAINING 9-12 WEEKS

FLIGHT TRAINING ABOUT 2 YEARS

MILITARY SERVICE 8-10 YEARS

Pilots learn in classrooms, cockpits, and flight **simulators**. They learn about rolls, **formation flying**, and flying upside down. After earning their **wings**, pilots practice advanced moves like flying close to the ground.

Fighter pilots work together. Sometimes Air Force pilots will fly with the Navy. They work to improve the planes. Their bravery helps keep soldiers safe!

EAGLE EYES

Pilots must have perfect eyesight and excellent hearing. They must also be strong enough to fight g-forces without passing out or throwing up.

Fighter Pilot Wanted!

LOOKING FOR SMART, ADVENTUROUS PEOPLE TO FLY THE WORLD'S MOST ADVANCED FIGHTER JETS

EDUCATION: COLLEGE DEGREE

EXPERIENCE: NO EXPERIENCE NECESSARY; TRAINING PROVIDED BY AIR FORCE, NAVY, OR MARINES

QUALITIES:
- PHYSICALLY FIT
- GOOD AT STAYING FOCUSED
- STRONG LEADERS
- TEAM PLAYERS

SALARIES FOR THIS POSITION CAN REACH MORE THAN $120,000!

Glossary

altitude—how high up something is

careers—jobs people do for a long time

cockpit—the small space in a plane where the pilot sits

eject—to be thrown out by force from the inside

formation flying—two or more aircraft flying together in a preplanned, coordinated way

g-forces—the pull of gravity on a pilot's body while they are in the air

missile—a weapon that is shot at a faraway target

missions—military assignments

scramble—to move quickly with purpose

simulators—tools that let someone experience a situation under conditions similar to real-life

surveillance—a mission in which pilots keep close watch on something to gather information

wings—a patch showing wings that goes on a fighter pilot's uniform; pilots earn their wings when they finish flight training.

wire trap—a system for helping jets land on an aircraft carrier; fighter pilots try to catch the aircraft's hook on one of three wires to stop.

To Learn More

AT THE LIBRARY

Omoth, Tyler. *Fighter Pilots in Action*. Mankato, Minn.: Child's World, 2017.

Snedden, Robert. *Air Force*. New York. N.Y.: Gareth Stevens, 2016.

Spilsbury, Richard, and Louise Spilsbury. *Aircraft Carriers at Sea*. New York, N.Y.: Rosen Publishing, 2018.

ON THE WEB

FACTSURFER

Factsurfer.com gives you a safe, fun way to find more information.

1. Go to www.factsurfer.com.

2. Enter "fighter pilot" into the search box and click 🔍.

3. Select your book cover to see a list of related web sites.

Index

Air Force, 6, 7, 8, 12, 20
aircraft carrier, 5, 8
bases, 4, 8
Blue Angels, 12
bombs, 6
career path, 19
careers, 18
checklists, 10
college, 18
dogfight, 14
gear, 16, 17, 18
g-forces, 15, 16, 20
job posting, 21
Marine, 7
military, 6

missile, 4, 6
missions, 7, 8, 11, 12
Navy, 7, 8, 12, 18, 20
Officer Training School, 18
planes, 4, 5, 6, 8, 10, 14, 20
practice mission checklist, 13
scramble, 11
Shults, Tammie Jo, 9
study, 8, 12
surveillance, 12
Thunderbirds, 12
train, 8, 12, 14, 18, 20
United States, 7
wings, 20
wire trap, 5

The images in this book are reproduced through the courtesy of: Emre Umurbilir, front cover (hero); guvendemir, front cover (jet); Everett Collection Inc/ Alamy, p. 4; BotMultichillT/ Wiki Commons, pp. 5, 19 (top right); U.S. Department of Defense Archive/ Alamy, p. 6; Derek Gordon, pp. 7, 8; Andrew Davidson/ Wiki Commons, p. 9; Aviatrix8704/ Wiki Commons, p. 10; picture alliance/ Getty Images, p. 11; Graham Moore/ Alamy, p. 12; Michael S. Murphy/ Defense Gov, p. 13 (top); Christopher Maldonado/ Defense Gov, p. 13 (top middle); Piotr Zajc, p. 13 (bottom middle); DVIDS/ Defense Gov, p. 13 (bottom); StockTrek Images/ SuperStock, p. 14; RGB Ventures/ Alamy, p. 15; Steven May/ Alamy, p. 16; Jaroslav Maroavcik, p. 17; Stephen Barnes/ Military/ Alamy, p. 18; g-stockstudio, p. 19 (top left); Joe J. Cardona Gonzalez/ Defense Gov, p. 19 (middle left); Joe W. McFadden/ Defense Gov, p. 19 (middle right); Ryan Fletcher, p. 19 (bottom); Matt Cardy/ Getty Images, p. 20; 94th Airlift Wing/ Defense Gov, p. 21.